To Jenny
+ John God
Bless
love
from
Jeff
xx

The Psychic Postman

Letters by Day,
Messages by Night

GW00726801

Jeff Phillips

www.facebook.com/ThePsychicPostman

This book is dedicated to Spirit

Acknowledgements

To my sister, Julie Aldridge
for writing my biography
and
to my girlfriend, Amanda Terrington
for her help with editing this book

Foreword

It has been at least six years since I asked my brother Jeff if I could write his story. He was hesitant at first but gradually conceded that it might be a good idea. The trouble with my brother is that you can never actually pin him down long enough to talk it through. His diary over-flows with church bookings, running workshops and offering his services at charity events.

After much persuasion from me and the promise that I would cook him a roast dinner, he finally found some time to pop over to my home where I could take some notes and recordings of his memories and outlook of his spiritual beliefs. This was when I learnt that my brother's memory is not what it was. I quickly acquired the art of interviewing, jogging his memory with events that I remembered. Our brother Simon was also asked of his memories about the early days until I finally had enough to start writing.

Each time Jeff came over to my house for another session, his enthusiasm grew and he was able to recollect more stories of his eventful life.

There is a part of Jeff's life that had been locked in a cupboard and the key thrown away, and I know that it took a great deal of courage for Jeff to release the dark past and let it fill a few pages of this book. It needed to be told, because without it, his story would be incomplete. It gives hope to everyone that no matter how bleak your life may be, spirit will shine a light for you to follow the path to happiness but they always need you to take that first step onto the path.

Even though I first thought about writing this book six years ago, it really wouldn't have been the right time. If you have a dream hold on to it, never let it go, because when the time is right spirit will shine that light for you to achieve your goals. This is my first book but I'm not going to say my last.

Thank you, Jeff, for giving me the opportunity to achieve one of my dreams.

Love Julie xxx

Brother and Sister
working for Spirit together.
Jeff Phillips and Julie Aldridge

The Psychic Postman

Awareness 1

Beginnings 5

First Steps to my Psychic Life 9

Finding Myself and Friends 12

Receiving Healing 18

Giving Healing 23

The Road to Clairvoyance 28

Church Services 33

Working for SAGB 45

A Friend comes Back 49

Opportunities 52

Charity Work 61

The Big Drip 66

Readings 68

Theatre 79

Ghost Hunting 82

Coincidences 85

Seeing Spirit 87

Predictions 89

Spirit Guides 95

Mother Nature 100

Does Money Interfere with True Spirituality? 104

The Jehovah's come Knocking 106

How the World of Spirit Works 108

Reincarnation 110

Shamanic and Pagan Teaching 113

A Message Retold 115

Happiness 119

Awareness

Flames smashed through the window, gasping for oxygen to fuel their growth. They spread up and across the guttering to chase the thick black smoke billowing through the roof tiles. I stood in shock on the opposite side of the street, hesitant to move towards the burning house, as the heat licked my skin, threatening to consume me where I stood. Looking down the street, a fire engine headed towards the fire. I noted that this fire engine should be speeding towards the uncontrolled flames, but it seemed to be moving in slow-motion, as if the driver was out for a leisurely ride rather than racing towards an emergency. The blue light was flashing on top of the cab but I couldn't hear the sound of its siren. The roaring of the fire was muted, soundless. Feeling overwhelmed with confusion, I glanced down the street and saw an elderly man and his dog walking towards the park and I heard the dog bark at a passing cyclist. I could hear the cars moving at the end of the street and the laughter of two women chatting outside their homes. Looking back towards the burning house, I now saw a child running from her home towards a blue car parked outside. The child's mother was calling to her daughter to wait for her. She picked up a toddler and followed her daughter towards the car. The pretty house was newly painted, there were birthday cards displayed on the living room window ledge. The upstairs window was slightly open, but the flames had been replaced by the lace of white net curtain, fluttering in the breeze. I came to my earthly time and realised I just had a premonition.

I shifted the heavy bag on my shoulder. I glanced down at the letters in my hand and noting the number, walked up to the door, pushing the letter quickly through the letterbox as I heard the dog scamper towards my fingers. Dogs and postmen are not always the best of friends. Turning back down the street to my next delivery, I took in the scene of a typical Monday morning in a North London street. People rushing to get to work, teenagers strolling to school. The sun was peeking out through a light cloud, promising to be a warm spring day. Not a house fire in sight.

I had been shown a fire that was yet to come. I wanted to cross the road, and stop the mother getting into her car, to warn her of the danger she and her family faced. I took a step, but I was unwilling to face the obvious reaction I would receive. The mother would probably call me crazy, she would feel threatened by this mad postman telling her that her beautiful home would soon be destroyed and her children's lives were at risk. What could I say to convince her? I had no idea of the timing of this event, it could be tomorrow or could be next year. There was the possible threat that I would lose my job if she reported me. Reluctantly I turned back to the job in hand and trudged up the path of the next house feeling depressed and helpless.

Over the following days, I continued my post round, each morning dreading turning the corner that led me down the street towards the place of destruction. A couple of weeks later, I saw the house, now destroyed by fire. I grasped for breath and had to hold a garden wall to steady myself. I knew this was going to happen but the shock of seeing the devastation brought tears to my eyes. My concern now was for the family so I crossed the road and approached a lady who was emptying her bins.

"Excuse me, do you know if the family are safe? Was anyone hurt in the fire?"

"Everyone is fine", she said, "It happened during the day, when everyone was out. I don't know the cause of the fire." The relief swept over me. I thanked the lady and walked with a lighter step to my next delivery.

That evening, I dimmed the lights, lit a candle, closed my eyes and opened my mind to meditate and feel the closeness of my spiritual guides. I asked my guides not to show me anything whose outcome I couldn't possibly change. I asked them not to show me disasters or suffering. I asked for laughter and fun. I was more than happy to see positive predictions - outcomes that would bring upliftment to anyone feeling lost or lonely. I wanted to brighten the world not dwell on the darkness. I felt blessed to be able to work for spirit, but only in love and light.

My spirit guides did not let me down. They never again showed me anything that I couldn't control or do anything about.

Beginnings

My name is Jeff Phillips, aka, The Psychic Postman. Someone once joked "Letters by Day, Messages by Night" which is very true, although I enjoy giving spiritual messages far more than trudging the streets of North London posting letters. I was born in Islington, London, and when I was four years old my parents moved to Edmonton, North London where I spent the rest of my childhood. I have an older sister and younger brother. There is a saying that the middle child is always a bit different. That is certainly the case with me.

At home, there were the conflicting views of spiritual and atheist beliefs. My father and brother were complete atheists. They didn't believe in a god or spirits. My brother once said "when you're dead that's it, that's the end". My maternal grandmother, mother and sister were very spiritual, believing in enteral life, a life after death. My grandmother and mother would offer psychic readings to friends and family using tarot cards, playing cards and psychometry. I remember them doing the 'Ouija board' once, but the outcome of that was unpleasant and threatening and now my mother is opposed to anyone 'playing' this board. It can have devastating consequences, even for the trained psychic medium, as it can leave the connection open to unwanted spirit that can be emotionally very upsetting. My grandmother would sit and talk to the spirits who seemed to follow her around wherever she was. My father would become very agitated and angry with her, telling her to stop talking to herself. I knew he thought she was a crazy woman, so I decided to never admit that I could see the spirits she was talking to. The last thing I wanted was to have dad calling me crazy! I purposely ignored what I could see, shutting my mind down to them and eventually they stopped showing themselves. My grandmother never encouraged me to follow the family psychic line. She believed that this gift was handed down through the females in the family and looked to my sister to continue the work for spirit, but my sister in her younger days was absolutely terrified of seeing spirit and although she believed completely, did not at that time want much to do with it. My paternal grandmother was an atheist, but in the many years after my grandfather passed to spirit, she gradually accepted her daughter-in-law's beliefs, and towards the end of her life she gained a lot of comfort knowing she would be re-united with her beloved husband. *God bless Family.*

Throughout my teens and early twenties, I found it very hard to 'fit-in', I did have some good friends, but I was always at a loss to know what I was meant to be doing or where I was meant to be going. I was shy and became very introverted. I found myself withdrawing from my friends and family, leaving me feeling isolated and lonely. My only outlet was playing football or going down the weight training club. I failed at all my school exams but I did excel at most sports. I was a very good footballer and wanted to become a professional goalkeeper, but found I couldn't take the pressure, so that dream failed. Then I started weight training. Loved this, building my body up and entering body building competitions. I had a healthy diet, put on weight and felt better in myself. Alas, weight training had to go because I refused to take the drugs that would have enhanced my body mass resulting in me not being able to successfully continue competing in the body building competitions. In my head, I had failed again and I slowly slipped back into my secluded and isolated life.

Although I rarely saw spirit in my younger days I did have a great imagination. I would often go off for walks on my own and often ended up in Tatem Park, Edmonton. My favourite place in the park being the sunken garden. I would sit here for hours imagining I was in a grand castle with a huge banqueting hall where I would see figures from the past, seated at tables, feasting on the enormous amounts of delicious food that lined the tables. I would find myself climbing the grand stone stairs up to the top of the castle and talk to a wizard. I believe this was my imagination, but perhaps unknowingly I was meditating, allowing me to talk to my first spiritual guide. Or perhaps my great imagination was just me escaping from the realities of life and a world I found hard to adapt to. **God bless imagination.**

First Steps to my Psychic Life

A female school friend once asked me what my astrology sign was. I replied "The fishy one" and she just nodded her head as if she knew something about me but would not tell me what. This intrigued me and I decided to find out more about astrology.

In my late teens, I was walking round Covent Garden in London and came across a spiritual shop called Mysteries. I have no idea why I walked in but I felt comfortable as soon as I opened the door to the smell of incense burning. The shelves were lined with crystals, candles, pendulums, buddhas, aromatherapy oils and shelf upon shelf of books. I had no idea what any of these books were about but the astrology books stood out. They seemed to jump off the shelf towards me and I had a vision of a deceased school friend insisting I buy one of these books.

I read and re-read the book, making notes and finding that I naturally understood how this worked. In those days, you would often find me in the local pub, The Two Brewers in Edmonton. Here my mates got to know about my unusual reading material and I became the butt of their jokes. I took this all in good humour and offered to do an astrology chart for anyone who was prepared to have a go. One mate volunteered and I spent ages compiling the chart. I presented the hand-written chart to my mate who took it with a laugh and joked that it couldn't possibly make any sense. I didn't hear from him for a while, but soon after someone else asked me for a chart and before I knew it I was doing so many I couldn't keep up with them. Although I didn't get much feedback from doing the charts, I knew they must have been good or I wouldn't have had so many requests. I got fed-up with them in the end. Each chart would take two hours to do and to be honest, I'd rather have been in the pub playing darts.

In 1984, on one of my many walks around Edmonton, I noticed a poster in a newsagent's window advertising a clairvoyant evening at Alyward School. I decided to go to see what it was all about. I was very apprehensive and crept in trying not to draw attention to myself. I sat right at the back of the hall and sunk down into my chair with shoulders hunched, wanting to watch without being seen. The medium giving the demonstration was Marie Taylor. She went from person to person giving evidence of eternal life, and each of them receiving their message would nod their head and thank Marie for connecting with their love one in spirit. At the end of the evening she pointed at me and said "All I have to say to you is go to your nearest spiritualist church". I nodded my head, sinking further into my seat as everyone turned to see who she was speaking to.

Later that evening, I reflected on what Marie had said. At school, I had had a small interest in religious knowledge but I was not a religious person, for it seemed you had to be holier-than-thou and perfect, which I most definitely am not. I searched the telephone directory, found my local church - Edmonton Spiritualist Church - and resolved to go the following Sunday. I was nervous as I rode my bicycle to the church, but as soon as I got outside I had an overwhelming feeling that I belonged here. I don't know why but this is how I felt. I didn't know what to expect, but I crept in and again sat in the back row. There were a lot of people there. We sang a couple of hymns before the medium gave a talk and then she went into clairvoyance. I enjoyed every minute, at last I found where I was meant to be! **God bless Marie Taylor.**

Finding Myself and Friends

I continued to go the Edmonton Spiritualist Church. Although extremely shy and introverted I did make some lifelong friends. Les and Jackie Fuller encouraged me in those early days and we are still great friends - socialising, and working together, holding shamanic workshops. Les used to play in a rock band and they would often invite me to go along to watch him in a local pub. Jackie and I sat with our drinks waiting for the band to play and no matter how much Jackie tried, she could hardly get a word out of me. I have no idea why they remained friendly with me, but I am so thankful that they did. Other great friends I found are Tom Flynn and John Reilly.

When I first attended the church on a regular basis, my new friends gave me the nickname of 'The Ghost', as I continued to creep in, sit at the back and as soon as the service finished, I 'ghosted' back out again, in the hope that no one would see me. To this day, I have no idea why my friends sought me out. My shyness and feelings of unworthiness convinced me to avoid them as much as possible. My thoughts were 'why would they want to talk to me?' When I think about it now, I'm sure that spirit was working behind the scenes, influencing all the church members to not give up on this lonely young man, and find a way to connect with him. After many months, perhaps more than a year, I started to get involved in the church activities. Before each service, I would put the chairs out and run errands. I would help tidy up after the service and basically get involved any way I could. If the church members could get close enough to me to ask for help, then I would, but I couldn't just offer to help without being asked, my insecurities would leave me hesitant and believe that nobody would want me involved. **God Bless all my friends.**

I met some wonderful people at church. One lovely lady called Muriel became a very close friend. Muriel only had one arm, she lost her other arm in an accident in her Fathers factory. This didn't stop her from living her life to the full. Muriel was a Quaker and a fascinating medium giving one-to-one readings. She loved cats and in the early evenings, you could always find her feeding the stray cats at North Middlesex Hospital. She always knew when it was going to rain because her stump arm would tingle and she would say to whoever was with her "don't forget your umbrella". She boosted her pension by selling a range of spiritual items at the Psychic Centre Alyward School. Muriel took me under her wing, and I used to go around to her house where she would make us some dinner, and then light the coal fire and we would just sit and talk. They were very simple evenings, but for me it meant everything that this lady wanted and enjoyed my company. I still feel that the simplest of things in life are often the most important. Back then, just looking at the coal fire on a Saturday evening in the company of a special friend meant the world to me. We would chat about many subjects, not always spiritual, but the one thing she didn't know anything about was football. Now I love my football and I asked her who she thought would win in the Cup Final, Wimbledon or Liverpool? I told her that one team played in blue and the other team in red. She said the team in blue would win 1-0. I personally, along with the rest of the country (apart from Wimbledon fans), didn't think Wimbledon had a hope in hell, Wimbledon were ranked as the outright underdog. It wasn't a matter of them losing, but a matter of how many goals they would lose by! Result: Wimbledon 1, Liverpool 0. **God bless Muriel.**

Mary Mason was the president of Edmonton Spiritualist Church. She too became a close friend. She was from Yorkshire and was a very strong character. Mary had a heart of gold but she didn't suffer fools lightly and if you felt brave enough to cross her, be prepared for the quick of her tongue. Mary loved her garden and she asked me to help her out with some heavy digging. In return Mary would cook me dinner. Well never one to turn down a home cooked meal, I agreed although secretly I didn't think my digging skills warranted such high payment. The following Saturday afternoon I arrived at her house and Mary showed me into the garden. "Can you see them Jeff?" she said.

"See what?" I replied.

"Can you see the fairies? They are on the lawn". Well I looked for these fairies, but no matter how I tried, I couldn't see them. Mary said "You're not looking in the correct dimension. You have to believe to see in the correct dimension". I pondered over this and she was right, I didn't believe in fairies. Mary said "instead of saying 'I believe it when I see it', you have to have the belief first. When you believe, you will see in the correct dimension. That's how Mediumship works. Believe and you will be able to gather momentum and then see."

I just wasn't on that elemental level at that time. I have to say I have seen one or two fairies since then.

On one occasion I bought a healing wand from a spiritualist shop. I was drawn to buy it and was told that it had been hand made in America by someone living in the mountains. It 'contained the energies of the mountain'. I don't know how true this is as I could have just fallen for the sales pitch, but I became quite attached to my wand and I carried it around with me all the time. Mary admired my wand and made me a pouch to keep it in. Now when anyone asks about my wand, I always tell them that the wand is wonderful but the pouch that carries it means more to me. It was made with love.

On another occasion, I was sitting with Mary in the back row of Edmonton Spiritualist Church watching the medium Doreen Stephenson work on platform. Mary psychically tuned into Doreen and was able to tell me exactly what message Doreen was going to give next. Mary said that Doreen would talk about someone who had passed to spirit by hanging themselves. The very next message was from someone who had committed suicide by hanging. The next message was about a car accident which Mary had correctly told me just before Doreen gave the message. Then Mary spoke of someone who had entered the spirit world after suffering a long illness. Again, Doreen gave the same message. This continued throughout the service, tuning into every message just before it was given. I was astounded. I had no idea that Mary was such a fantastic medium. She very occasionally worked on platform, and as far as I knew did not give many private readings. I only saw her help run the church and offer healing to those in need. Many mediums sit in church services and try to tune into the medium working on platform, but I have never seen anyone do it with such accuracy. It was astonishing. **God bless Mary and the fairies.**

Receiving Healing

A big part of the spiritualist church is offering healing. No charge is made for healing, anyone can request it, you don't need to be a member of the church to receive healing. My friends at the church could see I needed healing and although at first, I was reluctant to seek help, I decided it couldn't do any harm. In fact, I really didn't think it would work. At that time, I was in a very bad place.

In the years prior to me finding my spiritual path, depression had set in. Due to my lack of self-worth and self-belief and feelings of not fitting in anywhere, I stepped onto the rollercoaster of suicidal thoughts. I could not understand why I was meant to be here, so I might as well not be here. In the midst of this depression, a close friend had died and I had become unemployed. In my troubled mind, I decided to go to Brighton to seek out an old friend. I left a note for my mum saying I was going to seek my fortune and left without saying goodbye. I arrived in Brighton and walked through the town, hoping to bump into my friend. Looking back, I realise how ridiculous this was. I didn't have his address but believed that by magic my friend would just appear, but when your mind is numb, rational thinking alludes you. After sleeping rough for a couple of nights, I returned to London. Not wanting to go home, I made my way to Waltham Cross, where another friend, Steve, lived. His mother, Joyce, answered the door and explained that Steve had moved out some time ago. My eyes glazed over as I stood staring at her and rocked from foot to foot, unable to turn away. Joyce took one look at me and realised something was not right and asked me in for a cup of tea. I opened up a bit to Joyce and she said I could sleep in Steve's room while he was away, on condition that she could telephone my parents to let them know I was safe. I stayed with Joyce for a couple of weeks, but my depression sank to a new low. I wasn't sleeping and managed to get some sleeping tablets from the doctor. Sleeping tablets swallow very easily with alcohol. When the tablets had gone, I stumbled out of the door, not wanting to die in my friend's home, not wanting Joyce to find me dead. I got on a bus and ended up in East London. There was no reason why I should head to East London. Probably that was just the destination of the first bus that came along. Eventually the police found me and took me down to the cells for being drunk, but before they locked the door, one of the policemen had a second thought and realised that I wasn't going to sleep this one off. I was taken to the hospital where I had my stomach pumped. While I was unconscious, my granddad, who was in spirit, came to me. All he said was "You idiot! It's not your time." The next morning my father was called to take me home. The nurse brought me my clothes that I was wearing the previous evening, and I had to go home with a ripped shirt with most of the buttons missing. I realised that the doctors must have torn my shirt off to apply CPR.

I received counselling afterwards. I don't feel it did me any good. I briefly answered the counsellor's questions but refused to talk about the reasons behind my attempted suicide. I remember being asked whether I heard voices I my head. I knew I heard spirit voices sometimes, but I wasn't going to admit to that, as I thought they would lock the door and throw the key away.

The spiritual healing, I received in church, was comforting, peaceful and simple. I didn't need to speak to anyone and unlike counselling, I wasn't being asked any questions. Spirit knew why I needed healing and that was all the healers needed to know. The healing power was channelled from spirit to the healer, and I received this energy from the Healer's hands. Receiving healing is a very calming and loving experience. It left me with renewed faith and love for the church and for all those who work for spirit. **God Bless all Healers.**

After my attempted suicide, my brother, Simon, made a conscious effort to connect with me. Knowing I loved my sports we both joined a basketball team. We never really played in competition, but we would turn up at Picketts Lock Sports Centre every week for training. Exercise is a great healer for the mind and creates a healthier body. This continued for about six months until the day I landed on Simon's toe resulting in his toenail falling off. We swapped basketball for table tennis and continued to play for a few years. We also joined a darts team at our local pub, the Two Brewers in Edmonton. There were eight of us in the team. The team captain was a guy called Chicken George who arranged many matches in the pubs of Edmonton and Tottenham. To be honest, we weren't the most dedicated of players. We played well, but it was really just something to do while we had a drink. There was one time when Simon and myself got through the pub stages of a competition, which led to the later stages of a darts tournament. We turned up at a hall in Tottenham where there was row upon row of dart boards. The other players were so good they looked almost professional with their expensive darts compared to our borrowed pub darts. We looked at one another and both thought "What are we doing here?" We got chatting to another couple of guys telling them that we had no idea how we manged to get here and we knew we would be going home after the first round. Our names were called and as we stepped forward, we found our opponents happened to be the guys we had got talking to when we arrived. Our opponents looked smugly confident as I took my first throw of the dart. Amazingly we won that first round leaving the opposition pretty upset and looking ready to settle the defeat in a very unsportsmanlike way. Simon and myself were pretty streetwise in those days and the guys soon packed their darts away and sulked back towards the bar. We got knocked out in the next round, but it was such a funny day and not one to ever forget. Other good times were had with this little team of eight, not so great, darts players but it all came to a close after the death of Chicken George. Unknown to us, he was depressed which lead him to commit suicide. I don't believe this affected me, probably because depression was something I lived with on a day to day basis without anyone realising and Chicken George just did something that was never far from my mind.

Those years of becoming involved in the church, and socialising in the evening with friends, helped me to heal and to realise that sometimes you have to come out of your comfort zone to attract positivity into your life.

Giving Healing

After receiving healing, I felt a little better in myself. I'm not saying that my depression was cured, for there were times when the blackness would return to haunt me, but I found that I could summon the courage to fight back. I wanted to live and I wanted to be happy. The church was my rock, it gave me something to hold on to in those desperate times. I would breath in the love that hung in the air like an invisible power, and I gripped this power as my life support.

Wanting to give something back in return for the support and comfort I received, my thoughts turned to helping other people who were unwell whether physically or emotionally. I still felt uneasy around people and my lack of self-belief couldn't shake off my notion that other people would laugh and dismiss me. Absent Healing seemed to be the best path for me, as I would not have to come into contact with the person I was sending healing to. I convinced myself that I couldn't possibly let anyone down apart from myself and I had let myself down so many times that one more time would be insignificant in the grand scheme of things. Each night I would send out loving thoughts to people who I knew were ill or in an emotional turmoil. One of the church members, Keith, was suffering from cancer and I asked his permission to send him healing. He was a very spiritual person and understood the positive results that he would receive. He agreed, but I did not tell him when I would be sending the healing. One evening, I filled my mind with loving thoughts for Keith, and in my mind's eye I could see him in bed reading a book. I continued for the next hour, just visualising him and surrounding him with healing light and sending him positive and loving thoughts. The following Sunday, I met Keith in church and he told me that he knew I was sending healing to him while he was in bed reading a book. I thought this was a bit of a coincidence and didn't understand how he would know, so I challenged him and said "If you really saw me when I was sending the healing, what was I wearing?", knowing he couldn't possibly guess. Keith looked at me and said "you made me laugh Jeff, you were only wearing a shirt, and was completely naked from the waist down". We both roared with laughter. This was completely true, I sent the healing half way through getting undressed for bed. I didn't cure his cancer but I sure brought some laughter to his troubled life at that time. *God Bless you Keith.*

It was after this time of absent healing that I started to grow in confidence and wanted to explore the practice of spiritual hands on healing. This type of healing involves placing hands on the patient's head while they are sitting, and channelling 'energy' from spirit, through the healer to the patient. To do this I had to study for my S.N.U (Spiritualist National Union) certificate. Now I'm not one for studying and I don't really believe in getting papers and passes, but in order to work with hands on healing, I had to get this certificate in order to get insurance. Actually, passing this certificate increased my confidence a bit more and I started to offer healing at the church. I have seen miracles with other healers, but as far as I know, no one was miraculously cured by me. Patients used to say they felt a bit better, but I believed they were just saying that to make me feel good. None the less, I soldiered on and I found that by engaging with people I started to open up and developed rather an eccentric personality. The healing itself is a very intense and focused event but before and after the healing, patients need to feel relaxed and happy. My conversations with them were always on a lighter vibration and patients would laugh at my quips and walk away feeling positive and uplifted. People started to compare me with Frank Spencer, a hilarious charter from the TV programme 'Some Mothers Do 'Ave Em'. I rather enjoyed this comparison, I could laugh with them and learnt not to take myself too seriously. I loved hearing the laughter and believe that laughter is the best medicine, it can uplift your mood and bring positivity into a negative situation.

I have always felt a closeness to animals, they don't judge you, and if you show them love and affection they will be your friend for life. I have a great love of cats and although I have never owned a dog, I once thought I might like to be a police dog handler. Animals were often brought into the church for healing (cats, budgies, dogs and rabbits). Whenever an owner brought their pet in, the other healers would pounce on them, I was never quick enough to offer my services. Everyone wanted to send healing to a beloved pet. One day a lady brought her cat in for healing. This cat was in a very sorry state. Its fur was falling out in large clumps, leaving the exposed skin sore with infection. There was pus seeping out of its ears, eyes and mouth and it really didn't look like it had much time left on this side of life. The other healers took a step back, nobody wanted to touch this bedraggled cat. This was my chance, I walked forward and volunteered my service. I stoked the cat and channelled the healing 'energy', and after the healing the owner put the cat onto the floor and it walked four steps forward before it fell over. The owner said "That's one step more than then usual Jeff, it usually takes three steps before falling over"! I think they were just trying to make me feel better. **God bless that cat.**

Jean, an elderly lady who attended the church regularly, fell so ill it was impossible for her to get to the church. Once a week I would cycle to her home to see how she was, make her a cup of tea and talk about the goings on at church. I would offer healing and she would always accept it and I knew it brought her a sense of peace. In church some days later, I heard that she had returned home to spirit and I was shocked to hear that she passed only two hours after I gave her healing. This really upset me, I looked at my hands wondering if I was channelling the wrong energy, I started to doubt my abilities and considered not offering healing anymore. My insecurities returned until a couple of weeks later when I was watching a mediumship demonstration where the medium connected to Jean and said "this lady wants to thank you for all the healing you gave to her, she says that your healing eased her transition from the earth plane to spirit". This taught me a vital lesson that healing is not all about miraculous cures, it's about compassion, peace, comfort, hope, upliftment and knowing the love of spirit. *God bless you Jean.*

The Road to Clairvoyance

I continued to give healing for about 5 years. I was growing more confident and happy as the years passed, and I got friendly with a lady called Judy who ran a circle at the church. A circle is a small number of like-minded people who regularly get together (usually once a week) to learn about the art of mediumship. Judy had watched me grow in confidence with my healing. She recognised that the shy, introverted young man was now laughing and joking with everyone. Young, old, rich and poor, she noticed that I held no prejudices against anyone and everyone was drawn to me. Judy thought I would be a great ambassador for spirit.

Judy approached me about joining the circle. I was interested in clairvoyance but all I wanted to do was my healing and told her so. Judy wasn't going to take no for an answer and persuaded me that I could join the circle to do my healing. On the first night of circle I sat down expecting to be asked for some healing, but found I was joining in with the others. I surprised myself in being able to connect and give messages to the circle members. At the end of the evening Judy asked me if I wanted to attend the next circle, but she would totally understand if I refused. I said "Are you joking? I'll be back. I enjoyed every minute of it."

In 1991, after a year in circle, Judy asked me to take a service on platform at Edmonton Spiritualist Church with her, as she thought I was ready to do this. I didn't hesitate, although nervous, I looked forward to it with anticipation. I loved every minute of that service, afterwards Judy told me she couldn't take me any further and I needed to spread my wings and go for it.

I don't see myself as 'gifted', I just really enjoy and have a passion for what I do. It's like being a painter, dancer or a builder, if you have a passion for something then you are meant to be doing it. I really enjoyed my football and weight training, but things got in the way, so you know you are not meant to be doing it. You just have to go out there and find another passion and don't give up. I feel so fortunate to have found the thing I like doing best and the icing on the cake is that this is something that I hope helps people. **God bless Judy.**

I began by taking a couple of clairvoyance evenings at Edmonton Spiritualist Church. I needed to move on to demonstrate at other churches, but nobody knew of me. I thought the best thing to do was telephone the churches, so I bought a psychic newspaper which listed a lot of churches and I phoned them asking for a booking or to put me on their reserve list, so that if they had a cancellation I would fill in for them. I started my clairvoyant journey going from church to church. I might not have been the best medium in the world but my love for spirit and working for those who have passed over filled me with joy and contentment. My eccentric personality came over in the services, so not only was I giving messages for people but they were having a good time. I think spirit liked my 'zany' personality where people laughed, cried and experienced many emotions, all of which uplifted them. In those days, some churches didn't like the laughter too much and in fact I was banned from one church because I was too funny. But as time has moved on, churches have become more relaxed and recognise that people want to enjoy themselves, they don't want to walk into a church feeling like they have to remain silent within a solemn atmosphere. Churches used to have many rules and regulations. I have been told to put my shoes back on when I slip them off to start demonstrating. I only take them off because I'm more comfortable not because it helps the mediumship. Some churches won't allow the medium to chat with the congregation after the service and some won't allow you to talk about reincarnation.

When I asked why discussing reincarnation was banned, one spiritualist church said there was not enough evidence to support it. What? Don't they realise that for many people there is not enough evidence about spiritualism? I would say 95% of spiritualists believe in reincarnation.

I remember that a ruling came out that a church could not display Jesus's Cross. There was uproar over that. Spiritualism welcomes all faiths into their church but if that church has its roots in Christianity, then they should be allowed to display the Cross if they want to. I would work for spirit under any religious symbol. Spirit have no boundaries. Dress code is another important factor. Churches like their mediums to dress smartly. Even today I know of a church that won't invite a medium back to demonstrate, not because their mediumship lacked evidence, but because he wore jeans and t-shirt. Personally, I really don't care what someone is wearing as long as the evidence is good and the congregation are enjoying the service.

Some churches have wonderful atmospheres and others feel rather dull with no atmosphere at all. However, spirit is spirit and can work whatever the atmosphere. I once served a big church in Watford which struggled to get people through the door. That night, there were only four people sitting in the congregation. My first thought was that I wasn't very popular here. My second thought was that this might be an early night. Still I connected to spirit and gave each of them an extra-long reading from their love-ones in spirit. There was even time to give my girlfriend a message which doesn't happen very often. **God bless all our churches.**

Church Services

Not all church services went to plan. At Uxbridge Church, I noticed a lady in the congregation that looked like she had dozed off. I spoke to her from the platform but she didn't respond, we were laughing that my messages must have been boring her. The person next to her tapped her shoulder to wake her up, but she didn't wake up, in fact she had passed to spirit world. Everyone was totally shocked no more so then me. I rushed to her side and took her hand, sending healing for an easy transition. Did she leave this world peacefully? I hope she did, with a smile.

Most churches light candles for the services and Potters Bar church was no exception. There were many candles on a ledge at the back of the platform where the medium stood. I was giving my demonstration when I noticed that the congregation were pointing at me and waving their arms. I just thought I must be working very well and I really did have their attention, but then I could smell burning and people starting shouting "Jeff, Jeff, you're on fire!". The candles had caught my shirt, and flames were coming from my back. Luckily there was a jug of water on the table that was meant for me to drink and the chairperson grabbed the jug and threw the water at my back to douse the flames. That did the trick and I carried on the service with half a shirt.

Basildon church had glass panels in the roof. It was a beautiful church and when the sun shone, beams of light would dazzle down onto the platform. As I began my demonstration we all started to hear banging noises. We looked around thinking that spirit was trying to get our attention in a physical way, when a stone suddenly came crashing through the glass panelled roof landing on one of the congregation. It was the local youths throwing stones up on the roof, but I continued to demonstrate, dodging the stones, while people were hiding in fear under their chairs. Eventually, a couple of men from the congregation chased the youths away and the service went on with a few holes in the roof.

Sometimes I travel quite a long way to get to a church and in the early days before I could drive I would take public transport. I live in North London and a South London church asked me to serve. Travelling by public transport on a Sunday, from one side of London to the other, can take hours so I gave myself plenty of time, allowing for a few delays, I'd rather get there early then late. On arrival at the train station, I was greeted by the announcement that the next train had been cancelled and I would have to wait thirty minutes for the next. "It's OK" I thought, "I've got plenty of time". Eventually on the train, I arrived at Liverpool Street and headed for the Tube to take me to South London. As I walked out of the tube station it started to rain and I needed to find the bus stop for the final part of my journey. It took ages to find the correct bus stop and when I finally boarded the bus I was soaked through to the skin. By now I knew I would be very late and would have to run the last leg of the trip to the church. I arrived twenty minutes late, and the church doors were locked. I could see a light through the window so I knocked on the door repeatedly until someone answered. Finally, a gentleman came to the door, and I apologised for being late and explained about my difficult journey. He replied "That's OK Jeff, we got someone else now" and with that he shut the door on me. There I was, standing in the rain not quite believing I hadn't been invited in to watch the other medium and dry off a bit. I shrugged my shoulders and turned to look for the nearest kebab shop.

I was invited to serve Southend Spiritualist Church, so decided to make a day of it. I took a stroll along the seafront and stopped to play in the amusement arcades. After a train ride to the end of the pier and back I was feeling a bit peckish and made my way back along the seafront to find a fish and chip café.

The food was delicious, and after drinking a couple of cups of tea, I made my way to the church. As I stepped onto the platform ready for service I felt a gurgling in my stomach. I asked the chairperson if we could delay the start while I went to the toilet. Returning back to the platform, my tummy still didn't feel too good, but I hoped I would be OK until the end of service. After the opening prayer, the chairperson announced the hymn to be sang and I quietly whispered in her ear that I would visit the little boys room while they were singing. They had finished singing and patiently waiting for me to return to platform to give the address. I explained that I had a little tummy upset but hopefully all was fine now and I would continue the service without any interruptions. How wrong was I! As I started my demonstration I had to excuse myself again. Running in between the chairs, heading for the back of the church, I asked them all to sing another hymn while they waited. Well by the end of the service most of the congregation were hoarse from singing so many hymns. Not many messages given that night but plenty of cups of tea to parch their dry throats at the end of the evening.

I was booked to do an evening of clairvoyance at Newquay Church in Cornwall. I arrived the evening before, so decided to spend the whole day on the beach before going to the church in the evening. It was a glorious day, so I took off my shirt and laid down on the sand for a little snooze. I awoke a few hours later, feeling a bit hot. I stood up and felt rather dizzy. I looked down at my arms and they were bright red, I looked like a lobster. I got back to my hotel and laid down on the bed to recover before heading off to the church. While I was doing my demonstration, everyone was very concerned for my welfare seeing how red I was. I looked like I was about to burst into flames at any minute. The chairperson kept topping up my glass of water and telling me to keep drinking. Somehow, I felt well enough to keep going, but it took my skin over a week to recover.

I was demonstrating in church when I was drawn to a young woman and said that her friend had told her that she had had enough of this world and she didn't want to be here anymore. The young woman was amazed and said "yes, that's correct". I told her that spirit were doing their best to intervene and try to help her think differently. I said "They are trying to help her become more positive about life". The young woman got her mobile phone out and said "let me show you this text that I received today from my friend". The text said 'thank you for being my friend, but I've had enough of life, and I'll see you in the next life.' For me this was pure evidence of eternal life and spirit trying to help where they can.

I've seen many odd things take place in church but one of the strangest was while I was giving a demonstration in Hornsey Spiritualist Church, London. It was a very popular church and when I arrived there were about forty or fifty people in the congregation. As I stepped onto the platform, I noticed that in the front row there sat a group of about six people who obviously knew one another. At the feet of a middle-aged women was a wicker picnic basket. I didn't notice them much until about half way through the service, when the women opened the picnic basket and started offering sandwiches to her friends. Out came sausage rolls, packet of crisps and finally a flask, and someone remarked how good the coffee was. I said "What you got in those sandwiches? Anything nice? I'm feeling a bit peckish". I laughed and continued with the service. The audacity! A picnic during a church service, I've seen it all now.

At Harlow church, I went to give a message to an elderly lady who was laying horizontally across a row of chairs. I tilted my body to the side so that I could talk to her properly but I found this quite awkward and asked her if she could sit up. She didn't want to, so I continued with the message as best I could until there was a shout from the entrance, "Everyone get out, the building is on fire!". I rushed to the horizontal lady and pulled her up, "quick, you have to get up" I said.

Once she smelt smoke, she rushed from her comfy space. Gathering outside we could hear the fire engine siren making its way to us. The firemen doused the flames, which were coming from a waste paper basket in the toilet. It seems some youths thought this would be a good idea. After the firemen pronounced that the building was safe, we all flocked back inside to continue the service. The elderly lady resumed her horizontal position across the seats.

I worked a few times at Stamford Hill Church. I can't remember why, but the Service always took place in the crypt and no matter how hot it was outside you always had to take a scarf, woolly hat and gloves. It was freezing down there. It was very strange to look out on the congregation dressed for a winters day when in fact it was 30° outside.

The following was told to me after a service, as I had no idea it was happening at the time. I was demonstrating in a centre, where there was a large union jack flag pinned to the wall behind me. I was giving a message to two young ladies sitting at the front, when suddenly their mouths dropped open and their eyes widened as if in shock. I couldn't think what I had said to cause such a reaction, but trusting that spirit were giving me great evidence I continued. At the end of the evening a man came up to me and said that while I was giving a message, the right-hand side of the flag behind me slid down the wall, and then went back up again. I looked at the flag, and it was just how it should be, but the man said he had taken a photo, and sure enough the flag was hanging down on the right side. We went up onto the stage and found the flag was securely stuck to the wall. A very active spirit in that centre!

There have been services where I haven't worked very well at all. I was working at Balham Church when a few people got up half way through the demonstration, and as they walked towards the door one of them shouted, "That was a load of rubbish mate!" I must admit I didn't think I was having a good night, and decided to make light of the situation, so I asked them if I could go with them as I agreed I wasn't on top form. The request was declined.

My girlfriend, Amanda, sometimes joins me in my services. She works as a psychic artist but will not join me on platform as she is a bit shy. She prefers to sit at the back of the church with her pencils and paper. While I am working, she draws an image of someone in spirit, and at the end of the service she hands the drawing to me. I tune into and link the image drawn to someone in the congregation. I give the message and present the portrait to the receiver. We have been quite successful with this way of working for spirit. The person who I linked to the drawing have always recognised the portrait and accepted the message. We plan to continue working this way in the future.

I am so pleased I have come across this way of life. It has brought me out of my shell from a shy man to an outgoing positive person. I have met people from all types of backgrounds and personalities. Some people think I should know all about everything. I have a small insight on a spiritual level, and my interests are psychic phenomenon and sport. I do not know what toothpaste is the best to use (yes, someone did ask me that once!) nor do I know what the winning lottery numbers are going to be.

I have been asked whether I think the spiritualist movement will grow, with more people attending church services, or if there is going to be a big uncovering of knowledge coming soon. Spirit have never told me that there will be an awakening soon. I find it hard to imagine that the spiritualist churches will be full to overflowing as they were during the second world war. I have seen photos of that era where the churches were packed to the rafters with people wanting to hear from family and friends lost during the war. Spiritualism will always bring comfort to those devastated by the loss of a love one.

I have always said that I'm not gifted or special. I'm a postman who happens to love working for spirit. It doesn't matter if I'm not number one or good enough for TV shows, all that matters is being a part of it, being on my pathway, striving to do my best, to be a good channel for spirit, that is all I can do. So, whether your love of life is mediumship, painting or bricklaying, do the best you can, enjoy and have a great journey. **God bless our life journeys.**

Demonstrating at the Beacon of Light Spiritualist Church
in Enfield

Waiting to start a demonstration

Demonstrating at the Lemon Tree Cafe

Bringing the laughter to a spiritual demonstration

Working for SAGB

I had worked at many different churches, halls, restaurants and pubs and wanted to work for one of the big spiritual organisations. I wrote to a few of them; The Arthur Findlay Spiritualist College, The Greater World Spiritualist Association and The Spiritualist Association of Great Britain (SAGB). The only reply I received was from the SAGB who said they were interested in testing me and I saw this as a great opportunity. At that time, I was young with long hair, I looked more like a heavy rocker then a professional medium. I made sure I was dressed smartly and tied my hair back into a pony tail and travelled into London for my interview. The headquarters of the SAGB was an imposing building on Belgrave Square and as I walked through the doors the place oozed history. I was met by an elderly gentleman who showed me to a small room where I gave a private reading to one of the staff. Then I was led into a small hall where I gave a demonstration in front of a small crowd. There were staff at the back of the hall with clipboards judging my demonstration. I wasn't told at the time whether I had passed or not, but I knew I had done my best and even if I didn't get accepted I could say I had worked for the SAGB at least once.

Within a few weeks, they wrote to me. My hands shook as I opened the envelope, a mixture of dread and excitement coursed through me. I need not have worried, I had been accepted to work there and I am eternally grateful to the SAGB for the opportunity. I learnt so much over the following years, meeting other mediums and giving readings to an array of people from all sorts of backgrounds, a few famous ones including politicians and TV stars, some I recognised, some I didn't.

One of the most extraordinary experiences I had while working for the SAGB, was when a couple walked in for a private reading, and they were followed by two aliens. I knew they were aliens because they certainly didn't look like any human I had ever seen. Their bodies were white, with huge black oval eyes. They didn't appear to have any legs as they moved by 'drifting' just above the floor. Now at that time I had never given much thought to extra-terrestrials and I had certainly not seen any aliens in any of my readings. I mean, I had thoroughly enjoyed the film E.T. along with the rest of the country, but whether I believed in life on other planets was doubtful. I did not see these two aliens with my physical eye, I saw them with my third eye so I knew they were either in spirit, or perhaps in another dimension that I had never been aware of before. I was feeling shocked and confused. There was a part of my brain telling me that I was hallucinating but another part telling me this is real. How on earth was I going to explain this to the couple. I had no idea whether to tell the couple about the aliens or whether I should keep quiet and just get on with the reading. I decided to keep quiet, but when I focused on spirit connections, my mind went blank. I could not connect. All I could see were these two aliens trying to get my attention, so in the end I told the couple "I'm sorry, you are probably going to call me crazy, but I'm unable move forward with your reading until I tell you that two aliens followed you into the room and they are wanting to talk to you." The couple looked delighted, "That's exactly what we have come to see you about. We can see the aliens, but we can't hear them." I was gobsmacked. Well this is going to test me. I made the connection clairvoyantly or perhaps telepathically and the aliens spoke of a project that the couple were working on and were unsure of their next steps in order to complete it. I told the couple that they needed to walk to the left of a building to be able to proceed with the project. They must not turn to the right. I had no idea what this project was about and I did not understand anything I was saying, but the couple excepted it all and said that it made perfect sense to them. The couple walked away from me very happy with their reading, and thankfully the aliens walked out of the room with them. I have not seen an alien since, but I am certainly more open to the concept of other spirit dimensions, spheres and mansions, and believe without doubt that there are indeed other forms of life throughout the universe.

Eventually I had to leave SAGB because of work commitments. I was up at 5am to work for the Post Office. Then I had to go straight into London for my work at the SAGB, giving demonstrations and private readings at 3pm and 7pm, arriving back home at 11pm, so I knew something had to give. Working for the Post Office was my bread and butter, it paid the rent, so regrettably I had to stop working for the SAGB. I have fond memories of my time there, it was a wonderful opportunity which enhanced my mediumship on many levels. **God bless the SAGB.**

A Friend comes Back

Before I became a postman, I worked as a stone mason for Blake and Horlock Funeral Directors. I worked alongside a lovely guy called Randolph, engraving the wordings on headstones. Randolph became a good friend. I was often invited round to his house, and as you walked through the front door the air would be filled with the rich smells of Jamaican food. My mouth would water as I spied the big pot on the stove and know that whatever was simmering away inside, it would be the best meal of the week. His wife and children were a delight to be with and they always made me feel comfortable and welcomed me into their home.

He was a good friend for many years and then I heard the devastating news that Randolph had been involved in a car accident that took his life. This wonderful, happy, upbeat man with a beautiful family taken so suddenly back to spirit, made no sense to me. My feelings were 'why him and not me?'. I wasn't married, no children and very few friends, I convinced myself that it should have been me, not Randolph. The day of the funeral came and the church filled to overflowing with family and friends, Randolph had so much to live for. It confirmed my sad thoughts of 'why him?' and it tested my faith to near breaking point.

I spent the following weeks in deep meditation which helped bring some peace and calmness. In one of the meditations I felt Randolph draw near and felt that he was saying that he was happy in spirit and would always be close to his family, helping to guide them along their life's journey without him. He said I would see him soon. I couldn't wait to see him. Wherever I went I would look for him, but there was never any sign of him. I became a bit despondent and dismissed the idea of ever seeing my friend again, but Randolph kept repeating in my head that I would see him.

Many months later I came across a disposable camera in the bottom of a sports bag which I hadn't used for a long time. I noticed that all the film had been used and although I couldn't remember taking any photos on this camera, decided to take it to the local chemist to have the film developed. When I went back to collect the photos the shop assistant told me that film was damaged and none of the photos had developed. She flipped through the images in her hand showing the black prints. Telling her not to worry, as I couldn't remember ever taking the photos, I turned to go, but as I reached the shop door, she called me back, "hold on, one of them has developed". Taking the photo from her, you could have knocked me down with a feather. There was my friend Randolph, looking up at me with a huge smile and a glass of beer in his hand – cheers! I was overjoyed. I was looking for him to materialise in front of me in spirit form but there he was in a photo that I couldn't remember where or when I had taken.

Sometimes things don't come about the way you expect them to. They turn out in the most unexpected ways – *God bless Randolph.*

Opportunities

I always say if an opportunity presents itself to you, take it! You just never know where it can lead to or what lessons you can learn from it. Spirit will always show new paths for you to take and you just have to fearlessly take a step and enjoy the journey. Sometimes these steps might not turn out quite the way you envisaged, but you will always gain experience and learn life lessons.

I have done a couple of appearances on TV. Channel 4 contacted me to ask if I would like to appear on the TV programme 'Banzai'. Banzai was a game show from Japan and they wanted to set up a psychic experiment. I wasn't particularly a fan of this show, but as I say, "always take your opportunities". I arrived at the TV studio and met five other mediums who were going to take part. We were blindfolded and sat in a row. When the music started, the presenter walked behind us until the music stopped playing, he would then stand behind one of us. Our job was to put our hand up if we thought the presenter was standing behind us. I tried but was not very good at it and was soon eliminated.

Another time a cable company asked if I would go to a restaurant in central London, to see if I could pick up on any spirit energies while they filmed me. On entering the restaurant, I knew that most customers liked to sit on the right-hand side of the restaurant. If a customer was sat in the corner on the left, they often felt uneasy and asked to be moved to another table. The restaurant owner confirmed that this was correct but didn't know why. I told him that a previous owner from many decades before had hanged himself on the opposite side of the restaurant and the oppressed energies could still be felt there, even to customers who would not class themselves as psychic. Before I left I prayed for the soul who took his own life and suggested that the owner contact a medium who specialised in psychic clearing.

I couldn't have been that great on TV, as I was never asked back again but I am glad for the experience. I learnt about TV filming and met some very colourful characters. It was fun, but not for me. My heart lies with the spiritual churches.

Edmonton Spiritualist Church asked me if I would be interested in running a spiritual circle. I had never thought of myself as a teacher, but I saw this as an opportunity to grow spiritually and hopefully help someone on their spiritual path. People attend a circle for different reasons, they don't all want to become platform mediums. Some just want to enhance their psychic abilities, some just need to find out more about the psychic life. I can't make people mediums or healers, I can only point the way by doing exercises which will bring out their psychic abilities and reach their goals. A couple of people have gone on to be excellent working mediums and are now off on their own adventures; Danny Wright, Roy Jones and Tony & Beverley Katz. Being in a circle is not always serious and we certainly had many laughs along the way. When a student feels like they are ready for working in the churches, I would ask them to join me on platform and we would jointly take the demonstration. Danny Wright joined me a few times and was increasing in confidence, so I asked him if he would like to join me giving private readings, at a client's house near to Alexandra Palace. When we arrived, we were greeted by the music and laughter of what was obviously a large party. As we entered the hallway we saw two tables and chairs and it dawned on us that we were to do our readings in the hallway. Danny felt like walking away, how on earth could he work in this environment. I reassured Danny that all would be fine, it's no different from working in a pub with lots of noise going on around you. "If you can work here, you can work anywhere" I said. I knew I sounded more confident than I thought. As we took our seats it soon became apparent that not only did we have to contend with the noise, we would also have to put up with party goers entering the hall to reach the stairs that took them to the bathroom. Danny gave me a look of resignation and plastered a smile on his face as he greeted his first client. As my first client sat down, I asked for her name. She answered "I don't know".

"What do you mean you don't know?" I asked astonishingly. Looking at her I realised she was so inebriated (or stoned) she couldn't even remember her name. "Well, how are you going to understand this message if you can't even remember your name?".

We got out of that house as soon as we could, and Danny, in a not very pleasant tone shouted "Don't you ever bring me here again!". I laughed it off and told him it was one of life's journeys, something to learn from. "The only thing I learnt here is not to accept any offers to join you in giving private readings at a party!". Danny went on to work in many churches and centres and is now a very popular medium. He is also happy to give private readings at parties.

Roy Jones joined me on platform many times. On one occasion, we were asked to take part in an evening of clairvoyance in Islington. When we arrived, the hall was full of women, most of them inebriated in varying degrees. Under the chairs were bottles of whisky, gin and vodka, most of them half empty. We started our demonstration, which was a bit hit and miss, and we couldn't wait to get out of there. We heard afterwards, that four phones were stolen and two fights broke out. I was relieved that we left the building before that happened. Someone contacted Roy and asked us to return for another evening. I insisted that no drinking was to take place before the event. The organiser agreed. When we arrived, we could see bottles of booze lined up on a table all ready for the disco afterwards. Most of the audience were sober and the evening went well. We did not stay for the after party. **God bless all my students.**

After a demonstration at a very popular church in London, a gentleman approached me and said he liked how I worked and he offered me a job that would take me all over the world as he had contacts in spiritual centres around the globe. It would be well paid and accommodation would be included. I got rather carried away with this idea and started to believe I was going to be an international star. It really was going to my head. The gentleman said there was only one thing I needed to do before he could offer me the job. I was intrigued and felt sure that I could do anything to accept his offer. He said "Jeff, I just need you to take elocution lessons". I was mortified, I couldn't believe he wanted me to speak differently. I declined his offer. I was cockney born, and I wouldn't be able to recognise myself if I started talking 'posh'. Well that was my world tour finished! Take your opportunities but don't change who you really are to please someone else.

Doing my mediumship work has taken me to places that I'm sure I wouldn't have otherwise gone to. I often go south to Cornwall to serve the churches in Newquay, Falmouth, Camborne, St Austell and Penzance. I have gone north to Scotland where all the congregations sing so loudly they could take the roof off! I regularly serve the churches in Norfolk including Norwich, Dereham and Toftwood.

Tom Flynn invited me to Ireland a few times, where we demonstrated in Cork and Dublin. Tom Flynn is very well known throughout Ireland. He has done many evenings of clairvoyance and been a guest on local radio stations. We worked in churches, halls, and private parties. The Irish are known to have a great sense of humour, but I don't think they were quite ready for me. Laughter in a spiritual demonstration didn't go down too well, but I hope to return to Ireland one day once I have retired from the Post Office.

A friend asked me to travel with her, to tune into the Vatican in Italy. The Vatican had been part of her studies and she wanted to see if I could pick up on anything. As soon as I arrived at this beautiful and amazing place, a priest from spirit immediately came close to me and gave me some information about the Vatican. I relayed this to my friend who confirmed all that the priest had said. The next day the pope was going to be at the square and although I am not Catholic I was waving to the pope with thousands of others.

My friend and myself visited Rosslyn in Scotland at around the same time that The Da Vinci Code movie was a big success at the cinema. Because of the connection to the movie there were a lot of people visiting the Chapel at the same time. I started to walk up the hill towards the Chapel and on reaching the top I looked over some fencing down onto the woodland below. I told my friend there was something very interesting at the bottom of the hill. I had an overwhelming feeling of being inside a cave. I could hear water dripping and I suddenly felt cold and damp. We decided to walk down through the woodland to take a look after we had finished our tour of the Chapel. How splendid the Chapel was with wonderful stained glass windows and symbolic carvings on the walls. There were some reporters from a Scottish Newspaper wondering around, asking people why they were visiting the Chapel and seeing if there was any link between the visit and The Da Vinci Code movie. A female reporter approached me and I informed her that my visit had nothing to do with the film, I wanted to see if I could tune into the building. She asked me what I meant by tune in and I told her I could find out about the place by using my intuition and third eye. She asked me if I would be willing to demonstrate this to her, so I told her I would tune into her. I told her that although she was here interviewing people she would rather be taking photos of horses. She looked at me astonished as she said that she worked for a horse magazine and would rather be doing that. Then I told her I could see the Swedish flag and that Sweden would be very important to her. She looked at me strangely and informed me that she had just been putting her family tree together and found out that she had relatives in Sweden.

When we left the Chapel, we headed to Edinburgh and found a spiritual shop. We got talking with the owners and they asked us if we had visited the caves in the woodlands at the bottom of the Chapel hill, just where I had said there was something interesting. I had forgotten all about it after talking with the reporter. Maybe next time.

There was once talk about travelling to the US, but alas this opportunity passed me by as I was concerned about giving up my job as I would have had to spend a long time over there. Yes, I am open to new opportunities but on a practical basis, I have to pay my rent! Perhaps when I have retired from the Post Office I could create a new opportunity for me to cross the pond. *God bless new opportunities.*

Charity Work

What I like doing most about my work is trying to give money back to those that need it. I have worked for many charities, from cancer to animal shelters. I love it. If anyone asks me to work at an event I will always do my best to be available. These charity events can be held in churches, halls, shops or even someone's home living room. It doesn't matter how big or small the event is, it always fills me with love and gratitude that I'm able to give something back to those less fortunate then myself. My mum, sister and myself regularly hold a charity event every Christmas for either Great Ormond Street Hospital or Noah's Ark Children's Hospice. This event takes place at my mum's home. We give one-to-one readings to friends and neighbours, with me working in the dining room, my sister in the kitchen and my mum in the study. This is a small event, but over the years we have raised a fair amount of money for charity.

I have worked with Roy Jones to raise money for Moonwalk Breast Cancer Charity, and I have worked with Danny Wright and Jackie Tarby at Cheshunt Spiritualist Church to raise money for a cancer charity. This event was called the 'Mad Hatters Tea Party', where we donned our costumes as the Cheshire Cat, Queen of Hearts and inevitably I dressed as the Mad Hatter. It was such a fun evening, I thoroughly enjoyed it. Reports of both these events appeared in the magazine 'The Spirit Messenger'.

A work colleague, Martin, had a young son, George, who was extremely ill with neuroblastoma cancer. George had all the treatment the NHS could offer him, but his outlook was looking very bleak. Martin had heard about some pioneering treatment being offered in America, so his family and friends set about organising many events to try to raise the money to get George to America for the treatment. When it came to my attention, I offered to do an evening of clairvoyance at Edmonton Spiritualist Church to help raise some money. Posters were made and displayed all around Winchmore Hill and Palmers Green Royal Mail Sorting Office. From those colleagues who didn't know about my personal activities, I was getting a few odd comments and became the butt of many good-natured jokes. This was drawing quite a lot of attention, and many colleagues pledged their support for the event, even if they did think it was a load of rubbish. I asked a spiritualist friend, Eva O'Brien to join me on platform, and the evening went really well. The church was packed with Post Office workers and everyone enjoyed the evening. I don't think I converted any of them to spiritualism, but Eva and me certainly opened a few eyes and gave them something to think about. Not forgetting the £1000 that was raised. The family eventually raised enough money to take George to America. Sadly, the treatment didn't work but before George returned to England, he spent a few very happy days at Disneyland.

Psychics and mediums sometimes get very bad press. We have been called charlatans and fakes, preying on vulnerable people. Although a couple of bad apples are out there, the majority of mediums just want to provide evidence of eternal life and offer upliftment and comfort to those suffering. If you have a private reading then there will be a charge. Mediums need to pay their rent and feed themselves just like anyone else. Many mediums offer their services to raise money for charity and to raise money for their local church. Mediums who work in the churches and centres are not paid, they only receive a small amount for their expenses. Offering their services for charity also opens the door for non-believers to find out more about spiritualism, as they come to support the charity, and often go away with an open mind on the work that mediums do.

One of the main charities I work for is The Lucky Horseshoes Sanctuary. I came across them when I bought a piece of land with the aim of holding psychic workshops and shamanic days. The sanctuary backs onto my land and I soon got chatting to Debbie Quy who runs it. I offered to help with the donkey's hay, food and vets bills, so now on my visits to church services you will find me rattling my collection tin collecting pennies for this lovely cause. Thank you to everyone who has supported me. **God bless all those in need.**

The Mad Hatters Tea Party with Danny Wright
and Jackie Tarby at Cheshunt Spiritualist Church

What a beautiful place to work!
Private Readings at The Faerie Festival, Capel Manor

The Big Drip

My partner, Amanda, introduced me to cycling. I used to cycle everywhere before I learnt to drive but had put my bicycle away the moment I brought my first car. We would often go for long bike rides to enjoy the countryside. I found it fun, and it gave me the exercise my body was definitely in need of. One beautiful Sunday morning, we took our bikes down to the canal. There were swans and ducks on the water who swam alongside us. Birds were chirping in the trees and butterflies danced around us. I caught a glimpse of a muntjac in the hedgerow and heard the bees buzzing around the wild flowers. It was so idyllic, I thought I was in paradise. I really couldn't have been anywhere better. Then all of a sudden it happened, without warning, my front wheel went over the edge of the canal bank and I was thrown, head first into the water with my bike following. After much splashing around I managed to place my feet on the bottom and stood upright, just managing to keep my head above water. After few deep breaths, I dived down for my bike and dragged it up out of the water, shoving it back up the bank. I hurled myself out of the canal unable to avoid the nettles that stung my arms, and I stood dripping wet. The first thing I tried to do is to act as if nothing had happened. A lady jogged by and I smiled and said "Good Morning", thinking she wouldn't notice the pool of water at my feet. But my hair plastered to my face and the wet weed clinging to my bike must have given the game away although I hoped she thought it was perfectly acceptable for me to take a swim with my bike. I got back on my bike and with Amanda leading the way (so that she wouldn't have to smell the rather unpleasant odour drifting from me) we continued our bike ride.

I asked spirit why they didn't intervene and warn me of what was going to happen. Their answer was "If you can't see a foot in front of you, you can't expect us to warn you of every calamity which just needs common sense to avoid". Well there you have it, so the moral of this story is 'even when you think you are in Paradise, always keep at least one eye open, especially when you are riding your bike along a canal'. **God bless Mother Nature.**

Readings

I have done thousands of readings over the last 30 years and I tend to forget most of them as soon as I've finished, but a few have stayed with me. I think sometimes I'm in awe of what spirit tells me, reinforcing my conviction to serve spirit in any way I can. I hope I help people on their life journeys and give evidence of eternal life, offering comfort to those left devastated by the passing of a loved one.

I gave a reading to a lady who asked me to go and see her. I didn't know her or her circumstances. As I tuned into spirit, a young man came forward in my mind and he told me his name and how he went over to spirit world. He said he was involved in a car accident and died at the scene, and that the lady in front of me was his mother. She confirmed that this was correct. The young man then went on to tell me that he wasn't the only one in the car, that there were three other people, and he told me their names. One female and two males. The lady got very emotional when I relayed the message and she confirmed that the names were correct. Although this lady was very upset, she told me that she was so happy to hear from her son and she now knew that he was still by her side in Spirit.

Working in pubs is not something I like to do. I find working spiritually while people are getting drunk not that easy to do and of course it is very noisy, so I do tend to struggle. But I like a challenge so when I was asked to do a pub demonstration I accepted it. As I started my demonstration I was drawn to a table where two couples sat. You could tell that the husbands had just been dragged along on this night by their wives, and they were laughing and joking and had very little interest in me or what I was doing. I was drawn to one of the gentlemen, and I could see in my third eye that his dad wanted to talk to him. The gentleman laughed and confirmed that his dad had passed over but he believed I had just took a guess. So, I asked his dad what his son had been doing that day and I told the gentleman "Your dad says you were cleaning your car today, and afterwards you put a 'For Sale' sign on it". The gentleman's face dropped and he confirmed that he had cleaned the car and put it up for sale. I have come to the conclusion that you sometimes need to tell people what they have been doing that day for them to think there is something to this. As I left the pub and said my goodbyes, the gentleman thanked me and I think I had a slight bit of respect for what I was doing and hopefully he was more open to spirit.

I was working at a centre doing one-to-one readings when a woman came to see me. As she sat down I instantly saw a black dog sit down beside her. I told her this and she immediately got up to go. I said "Where are you going? I've just started the reading". She said that her dog had died recently and all she wanted to know was that he was safe and well. The first thing I said had confirmed this and that was enough. I wish all my readings would go that smoothly!

I have spent some time in prison. Not because I received a guilty verdict, but because I was invited to give some private readings to the prison officers. It was very daunting walking through the gates of Holloway Prison, and I was shocked at the poor state of the accommodation that the female officers had to live in. I don't remember any of the readings being unusual, but it was quite an experience for me to be there.

I visited a work colleague at her home to give her a reading. Many of her family in spirit connected and she could accept all the evidence I gave. I then connected with her father, who I knew was still on the earth plane. I could hear him singing 'Tulips of Amsterdam'. My colleague could not accept this as there was no link with Tulips or Amsterdam. I was confused, but couldn't change the reading, so I asked her to check with her father. The next day at work, she approached me and confirmed that she now understood the song. Her father was singing it to a friend who was about to go on holiday to Holland. The time he was singing it was at exactly the same time her reading was taking place.

Another work colleague challenged me once and said that he could prove that all this spiritual stuff was a load of rubbish. He didn't believe in any of it and wanted to test me on a scientific level. I really don't mind that some people are opposed to what I do. Everyone has the freedom to believe in whatever they wish and I can only bring evidence through to encourage a different way of thinking. I agreed to the test and he asked me what zodiac sign he was. In my mind's eye, I could see a crab, so I answered "Cancer". He confirmed this but said that I had a one in twelve chances to get this correct and proceeded to ask "What number am I thinking of? I'll give you a clue, it's between 1 and 100." In my mind's eye, I could see the number 26, and told him so. He looked a little perplexed as this was the correct number, and then he put his hands behind his back and asked me how many fingers he was showing. He was showing two fingers of his left hand, but I was slightly unsure of the right hand. I knew he was either showing five fingers or his hand was in a fist with no fingers showing. I plumped for a fist, to which he laughed and said "No, I had five fingers showing, see I told you it was a load of rubbish!" I have come to the conclusion that no matter how many times you get things right, you only have to get one thing wrong to be branded a failure.

This has reminded me of another occasion after visiting the dentist for some major work on my teeth. I could see my dentist swimming. Now I normally keep things to myself unless the person has given me permission to connect, but in this instance, I asked the dentist if he went swimming a lot. He looked a bit taken back and told me that he went swimming every day in his lunch break. He asked me if I was OK, (he was worried that the anaesthetic hadn't worn off). I assured him I was fine and he said "I think you need to see someone Mr Phillips, why would you suddenly ask me this?" I have come to the realisation that even if you are right, some people are not interested and might think you are quite mad!

Sometimes I can give a reading and the recipient cannot understand it. As a medium, I would always ask spirit to repeat the message in case I have heard or seen it incorrectly. If I am sure that the message is correct, I will not dismiss it. This is an extremely hard thing to do, because when you receive lots of negative answers it's very easy to doubt yourself and become deflated. This happened in Walthamstow Spiritualist Church. A man who really didn't look like your average churchgoer, was sitting in the congregation. His arms were covered in tattoos, and he had the physique of someone who had spent many hours working out in the gym. The way he dressed, his stance and the lines on his face depicted a man who had spent his youth on the streets and he knew how to defend himself. I was a little apprehensive about going to him but spirit were insisting so I told him I had his grandfather with me and that he tells me he owned a snooker club. The man replied "Na, you're wrong mate, he never owned a snooker club." I told him a couple of other things, and again he told me I was wrong. Feeling a bit uneasy, I needed to move to someone else, so I repeated what spirit had told me and said that perhaps the man could check out the details with older family members. After the service, I could see this bulk of a man heading towards me and he raised his arm and said "Hold on there mate, I've got me mum on the phone, I'm gonna ask her about the snooker hall". Well to say I was a bit panicky was an understatement. Right there, in front of me, he spoke to his mum and she confirmed that his grandfather owned a snooker club when he was younger. The man turned to me and said "Well done mate, thanks for the reading". Relief flowed through me, I shudder to think what might have happened if I was wrong.

There's a great feeling when someone returns at a later date, after they couldn't understand a message and having asked in their family, they've confirmed what I have said. This puts to bed all those people who have told me that I'm a good mind reader. I really couldn't have been mind-reading when the recipient didn't know anything about it.

A young lady came to see me for a private reading. She was obviously pregnant, and I said she was going to be a bit disappointed with the birth because she had been told that her baby was a boy but spirit have told me that the baby was a girl. The young lady said that the baby was moving around so much when she had her scan that they couldn't tell her the sex of the baby. She had seen a number of mediums before seeing me and they all told her that her baby was a boy. She and her husband were delighted because they already had three daughters. The reading ended and a few months later the young lady came to see me. She told me her reading was correct, she now had a beautiful baby daughter and she couldn't be happier.

I went to the house of a middle-aged lady to give a reading. She was very pleasant and offered me a cup

74

of coffee before I started. About half way through the reading, a could see in the corner of the room, a pair of yellow eyes staring at me. The eyes were intense and seemed to penetrate my whole being. I was not comfortable, thinking I was seeing a demon. The angry eyes moved towards me and I immediately shut my third eye and closed down. I had never seen anything bad or unpleasant, and hesitated, uncertain how I was going to tell the lady sitting in front of me. I smiled at her and half laughing I told her I could see someone with yellow eyes that seemed to rush towards me. "Yellow eyes?", she replied. "I know who that is, that's my husband. He was an alcoholic and it affected his liver, so that his eyes turned yellow". I was half relieved that I hadn't seen a demon or the devil, although I knew he didn't like me being there. She said "He was a bit of a jealous person who didn't like anyone else in the house". I finished the reading, had another cup of coffee and went on my way.

I went to a gentleman while doing a demonstration, and for some unknown reason I asked him his name. Now I don't normally ask a client for their name but spirit were insisting that I asked. The gentleman told me his name but spirit told me this wasn't his real name. I challenged him and he admitted that the name he gave me was his pseudonym. I have to ask the question, why did spirit want to tell me he had another name? Giving messages from spirit is all about evidence and I can only presume that this evidence was what the gentleman needed to accept spirit in his life.

While doing a demonstration, I was drawn to a lady and said I could see her singing and dancing. I felt she was an excellent singer, and asked her why I could see Mick Jagger? I knew Mick was still alive and kicking, so I knew this wasn't a spirit form. She said that she used to be a backing singer for Mick and travelled on tour with the Rolling Stones.

When we pass over into the spirit world, our personalities remain the same or they show themselves to me as they were when on the earth plane. I was doing a demonstration and connected with a sergeant major who told me he wanted to give a message to a lady in the congregation. The lady understood the message, and then this sergeant major started to tell me off. He told me he didn't like the way I spoke, I didn't pronounce my words correctly, I was scruffily dressed and I should learn to stand up straight and not slouch. He also told me to get my dribbling under control! Laughingly, I relayed all this to the lady and she exclaimed "That's right, that's just how he was, that's him to a tee! I'm so sorry he is giving you such a hard time". Sergeant major was probably right with his assessment of me. It was so funny, everyone was laughing.

The spirit of an elderly lady drew near to me, and I told my client that this lady was taking a bird in a cage for a walk in a pushchair. I couldn't believe what I was seeing. But it was true, my client confirmed the story. Now that's not something you see every day!

It's always lovely to get feedback about readings. When I'm demonstrating I always try to bring in the fun and laughter. I'm honoured to receive many lovely comments about how funny my demonstrations are. After one service a lady approached me and thanked me for making her laugh. She explained that she had been very sad and lonely but tonight had been the first time she had truly laughed in five years. Although I couldn't remember her message, I thanked her and said that I was so pleased she enjoyed her reading. She replied "Oh, you didn't give me a message, I just laughed at everyone else's". Oh wow! Thank you, spirit.

I once had a lady tell me that she paid £100 to see a professional comedian, but she laughed just as much watching me for just a few quid!

If I can bring an evening of joy and happiness into people's lives without even giving them a reading, then I'm a lucky man. It's all I really want to do!

Theatre

I was asked if I would like to do a demonstration in a theatre with one other medium. I had never worked in a theatre before, but as I always say, if an opportunity is placed on your pathway, take it. The theatre was Castle Hall in Hertford which holds about 400 people. I was very nervous, as was my fellow medium, who stood outside chain smoking before being called to the stage. I prayed that spirit would connect with me. My family came along to support me, even my dad and brother who are both atheists and have no interest in spiritualism. I think the promise of an alcoholic beverage before and mid-way through the show enticed them to show their support. I was waiting in the wings, shaking, peeping out to the rows gradually being filled. It looked like it was going to be a full house. I was starting to lose my nerve when suddenly I heard my name being called as I was introduced onto the stage. I walked with a confidence that I did not feel, to the middle of the stage and looked out to the audience. The stage lights were on me and I needed to adjust my eyes to the dazzling brightness. I connected with a few people in the audience and my confidence grew and I could feel myself relaxing. I felt a grandfather figure from spirit stand next to me. He told me to talk to the women wearing a red jacket in the fourth row. I searched the fourth row and spied a young lady wearing the red jacket. "Hello mam, can I talk with you? I have your grandfather in spirit. He is giving me the names Tom and Jerry". I giggled to myself as a vision of the cartoon characters Tom the cat and Jerry the mouse came to view. "Can you accept these names?". She said she did understand the names. Her grandfather then told me that that Tom had been in trouble. In fact, he had been very naughty recently and the lady was quite upset with him. The lady burst out laughing as did those around her who obviously knew what this was all about. The grandfather wouldn't tell me anything else, so I asked the lady if she would explain. "Well Tom is a cat and Jerry is a goldfish, and Tom ate Jerry today! I was very angry with Tom and upset for the loss of Jerry". The audience roared with laughter and to me it felt brilliant. This is what I always want to do, bring laughter to my readings, spiritualism does not have to be such a serious subject. Although I felt a bit sorry for Jerry the goldfish.

After the show, I met with my family by the bar and my brother Simon said the evening was a bit of an eye opener for him. He concluded that there might be something to this because the cat and fish evidence was something to ponder on. I enjoyed my opportunity to work in the theatre and look forward to working at other theatres, but my heart will always lie with the spiritual churches and centres.

Ghost Hunting

I was asked if I could lead a Ghost Hunt in the De Vere Theobalds Hotel in Cheshunt. Parts of this hotel date back to the 15th century so it is steeped in history. A historian accompanied me as I walked round so that he could clarify anything that I said. As I entered one room I could see Winston Churchill sitting at a huge mahogany desk. He had many papers spread around him which he studied with deep concentration. The historian confirmed that this was the room Winston Churchill used as part of his war planning. Walking down into the cellar I could see many stretchers lined up against the wall, with white sheets covering the bodies. The historian confirmed this was used as a morgue during the second world war. While walking round I could pick up on rooms that were used as treatment rooms. I felt that the patients were sick in mind rather than having psychical injuries. The historian explained that world war two veterans were brought here suffering from post-traumatic stress disorder. I knew that these veterans had been locked up in many of the rooms after one of them had committed suicide by jumping off the roof. We then wandered outside into the grounds of the hotel where to my amazement an elephant lifted his trunk towards a tree branch and three camels walked leisurely in front of me. In the distance I could see deer and donkeys and to my right a lady dressed in Edwardian clothes climbed into a carriage that was harnessed with four zebras. As the zebras began to pull the carriage, the lady turned to smile at me, it was then that I noticed a banjo on her lap. I took a step back and asked the historian if this land had once been a wildlife park. He replied that it hadn't been a wildlife park but there had been a few exotic animals kept here. King James I owned this land and kept the elephant and camels here, and Lady Meux, an eccentric character, lived here in the late 1800's where she rode a carriage pulled by zebras and she could play the banjo extremely well.

On another occasion I entered a pub in Commercial Street, London and sensed a man who was not very nice. I believed he was quite wicked and knew that he had hid in the cellars of this pub. I also knew he died in prison. I had picked up on the spirit of Judge Jefferies, also known as the Hanging Judge.

Once, I was taken to a house in Finchley, London where Sigmund Freud lived towards the end of his life. As I entered the upstairs rooms I could see many children. I could see Sigmund Freud working with these children. I could also see a woman standing nearby. This was Sigmund's daughter who helped him with his psychology work. I didn't feel there was a lot of activity in this house, but I knew that while Sigmund lived here he became very ill with cancer.

I enjoy ghost hunting, but I like to have the evidence I give confirmed afterwards. I can go to many different places and see, hear or feel spirit showing me things from the past, but I'm not always satisfied until its verified by a historical expert.

Coincidences

Although I'm not a fortune teller and I don't make too many predictions, I just can't ignore coincidences where they have led to something amazing happening or indeed if it was fate that something should and needed to happen.

I was going out shopping with an ex-girlfriend, Pat, when she suddenly said that she needed to go to Edmonton Green to do the shopping. We lived in Epping at the time and I said "are you sure, that's really out of our way. Why do you want to go there? We haven't been to Edmonton Green for years". She insisted and to save an argument I drove her there. We finished our shop in the supermarket and Pat recognised her old friend serving at the till. "Hello Pat, I'm so glad I bumped into you. Carol is very ill in hospital with cancer and she has been calling out your name, but none of us knew how to contact you." Pat was in shock, it had been many years since she had seen her friend Carol, and to hear that she was calling for her, Pat knew she had to see her. Pat went straight to the hospital and spoke to her friend. Chatting about the old days with lots of hugs and kisses. The following day we heard that Carol had died that same evening. What were the chances of that happening? Coincidence? Some things are meant to happen. Spirit have a way of guiding your intuition even though you have no idea why. Pat had no idea why she wanted to go all the way to Edmonton to do the shopping, she just knew she had to go.

Seeing Spirit

Not all mediums see spirit with their physical eyes. Many see in their minds eye sometimes called third eye. The third eye is located in the centre of the forehead, just above and between the eyes. I normally see spirit using my third eye. I see images in my mind, often in colour, and I am able to describe that image to my client. I have seen two people seeing the same spirit, one using their third eye and one using their psychical eye. They both gave exactly the same evidence. So it really doesn't matter which eye you use when linking to spirit. When using the third eye you would know that the person or place you are seeing is definitely someone in spirit or a memory link that the client will recognise. I rarely see spirit with my physical eye, but when I do it can get quite confusing.

On a trip to Cornwall I visited Tintagel Castle. The legend of King Arthur is linked with Tintagel and I love the energy that surrounds the place. I took a walk through the ruins, then found myself a place to sit on the ruined wall of what was once a room within the castle. A man dressed rather oddly sat next to me on the wall. I said hello and commented on his historic clothes, thinking he worked at Tintagel. He replied

"No, I don't work here, I'm a poet. I like to sit here watching the ships sailing up and down along the coastline. I find it inspirational for my poetry". I agreed that this was a wonderful spot in which to write, and I turned my head to look down at the sea, thinking that it really was the perfect place for inspiration. I turned to talk to him some more, but he just disappeared in front of my eyes. Well I was completely taken by surprise and really didn't realise I was talking to spirit. I wanted to know more and made my way to the entrance to speak to one of the historians who worked at Tintagel. I asked him if he knew what the room was originally used for. He replied "That room was known as the Poet's Room". Wow!

Predictions

Sometimes, spirit show me things that are going to happen in the future. I'm not big on predictions. I don't like seeing future tragedies or misfortunes. I'd rather work on a lighter level to offer people upliftment and predict happy events.

In a private one-to-one reading, a young mother came to see me, and spirit showed me a new baby in her arms and this baby would be a girl. When I told her, a look of horror crossed her face. "There's no way I am having another baby. I have two young children and I am not planning to have anymore. We are struggling financially and another child would put so much pressure on us. You're wrong, perhaps it is a baby for my sister?" I could see she was getting quite distressed about this, so I decided to drop the subject and asked spirit to show me something that would uplift her. Three years later after the funeral of a family friend, a young mother approached me, and said "Hello Jeff, do you remember me?". I looked at her and searched my memory banks as to where I knew her from, but I couldn't recognise her face. She said "I had a reading with you four years ago. You said I was going to have a baby girl but I refused to believe you.

I was adamant that this wasn't going to happen and I got quite upset". I vaguely remembered, but with the hundreds of readings I've done, it's very difficult to remember individual ones. The young mother reached down and picked up a cute little girl who looked about two years old. "Let me introduce you to Sophie, my beautiful daughter. It was a shock when I learnt I was pregnant, but I wouldn't change her for the world. She completes our wonderful family. This is the baby you predicted". I looked into the mother's eyes and could see the love flowing from her for her baby. Spirit have a way of bringing joy to our hearts even when we don't know what will bring us happiness.

I was demonstrating in a shop in Ponders End, when spirit turned my attention to a teenage girl. I could see lots of tablets around her and I instantly knew these were not for medication. The girl was thinking or had even tried to commit suicide. This was a very sensitive subject and not one to be spoken about in front of other people, so I asked her to come and see me at the end of the evening. The girl did seek me out and I said I needed to be honest with her and said she would understand, that she is taking too many tablets. The girl nodded her head in silence, and I told her that her grandparents in spirit were asking her to stop because there were so many new options and opportunities she could take in the future. They wanted her to live and asked her to have faith that she would feel better soon. The girl left and I never saw her again. I hope that by spirit giving me this information, I was able to stop the girl from harming herself or worse, and she was able to seek the help she needed to recover.

Giving messages to people, whether on platform or privately, is a great responsibility. Mediums need to be tactful and learn to hold their tongue when receiving an unpleasant message. I work on a lighter vibration and do not get many messages about future disasters. I have seen mediums work on a much lower vibration, where they would predict horrific accidents and leave the client damaged and confused. I've seen a medium tell a client not to stand on a railway platform because someone will push them onto the rails. I also had a client come to me for healing after being told she would be involved in a car crash and although she wouldn't die, she would break many bones which would take many months to recover. This client wouldn't get in a car for two years. A medium who was demonstrating in a packed spiritualist centre told a woman in the congregation that he knew she had been abused as a child. The women became very upset and ran from the centre, crying. What type of spirit had the medium connected with to be given this information? A lower vibration, or the medium took a chance in singling out this woman for his fabricated story.

I actually believe that these mediums are not true mediums. They have not been trained correctly and when they are unable to provide true evidence, they make a story up and for whatever reason embellish the tale to shock the client. If these mediums insist that spirit are giving them the information then I suggest they seek spiritual healing to raise them from their low working vibration. Whichever way the message is received, no medium should inflict such damaging information to their client. The thing with giving predictions is what happens if you are wrong, what happens to your spiritual soul. I feel that your own soul is damaged along with your client's soul. No one needs to know that a plane is going to fall out of the sky. What can you do? Do you think the airline is going to cancel all fights that day? No. All you are doing is damaging lives by scaring the client so much that they refuse to live the life that was intended for them. I once saw a big ugly mark on a colleague's neck. This mark was not really there because I saw it through my third eye. I asked spirit how he would get the mark, and spirit showed me some stairs. A few days later my colleague came into work, saying he had fallen down the stairs and cut his neck on the banisters. There was the mark on his neck, just as I had saw it. Could I have stopped him falling down the stairs? No. He couldn't have stopped using the stairs indefinitely, so what would be the point of telling him before the accident happened. What was the point of spirit telling me this?

Luckily, the churches and centres are very mindful of these types of mediums and will not book them for their services. But it's difficult to police with private readings. If you would like to see a medium try visiting your local spiritualist church or centre. Entrance fees are normally very low and many will know of mediums in the local area. Psychics are a bit different in that they do not give demonstrations. Psychics will give readings to help you with your earthly situations. They do not connect to spirit. So, whether you are looking for a psychic or a medium (or both), try to see one who has been recommended. When looking on the web, check out their reviews, find their social media pages to see where they are demonstrating, and generally discover what other people are saying about them, before booking an appointment.

I ask spirit to bring me positive and happy predictions. I recently told a client that something wonderful would be happening on 14th September. She smiled and said she was getting married that day.

Yes! Positive and uplifting messages are all I want to give, and these messages come from spirit, not from me.

Spirit Guides

When I first started to open up to spirit through my healing, I became aware of a monk as my spirit guide. This guide helped me by being a calming influence. He represented stability, peace, and security from the outside world. He helped me with deep meditation and healing, and I loved his presence. After a few years developing on a healing level with my monk beside me, I became aware of a Native American Indian. Now I didn't want to change my guide, so I rejected this Indian. Spirit kept insisting that this new guide was here for my spiritual growth, but I continued to reject him. I even went to see a psychic artist and asked him to draw a picture of my spirit guide. He drew a Native American Indian, and still I couldn't accept him. Whenever a vision of this Indian appeared, I would turn my head away and close down my third eye.

I think spirit were getting a bit impatient with me and they told me that they were going to prove to me that I needed to accept this new spirit guide. Later that year I took a trip down to Glastonbury in Somerset. Not for the music scene, but because it is a very spiritual place. I feel totally at home there. It feels like

I have come home whenever I'm there. I was sitting in the beautiful gardens of Chalice Well, opening myself up to the solace and peace, when I could see with my physical eye a number of monks walking up towards Glastonbury Tor, where in ancient times a monastery stood. The lead monk held the cross of Jesus in front of him and the following monks were singing. Within five minutes of watching this scene, I looked back to the gardens that I was sitting in and suddenly a Native American Village appeared all around me. There were many tepees, and groups of women sat on the ground while the children ran between them. I could see horses on the perimeter of the village and a number of men standing in the centre were in deep discussion. I saw this scene so vividly I knew I had to accept that things were changing for me. This was spirit's way of proving to me that I needed to accept my new guide in order to further develop my spiritual path.

My monk had guided me through meditation, prayer, healing and solitude. Now my Indian would help me to connect with the love of family in spirit. He wanted me to develop hands on healing, to connect with people and start the path to mediumship. It was a very amical change from monk to Indian. I was changing from absent healing, that very solitary task which helped people in silence, to hand on healing where I would need confidence to talk to people. My monk was a recluse, and I was moving onto a very sociable path. I have no regrets saying goodbye to my monk, but I do have a tattoo of 'The Hermit' from the Tarot card deck, knowing he walks with me in my heart. My Indian's name is Two Feathers. My monk didn't have a name. In our lonely work, there was no need for names.

Not long after this change, I was invited to join a circle held in Hornsey Spiritualist Church. The circle leader took a leaf from a box and placed it in my hand. Now I don't feel 100% confident with psychometry but I held this leaf and tuned into it. Immediately it felt like the leaf was singing a beautiful melody to me. It was like nothing I had ever heard before. The energy from this leaf was so powerful and vibrant that I knew I had to have it. "I'll give you £100 for this leaf" I told the circle leader. "I'm sorry Jeff" she replied "I can't let it go". I needed to know more and asked her where she found the leaf. "This leaf comes from America", she said. "The tree it comes from is scared, where for hundreds of years, generations of American Indian tribes have worshipped, prayed, chanted, danced and sang around the tree. I was given it by a very dear friend who is of one of the tribes. I really couldn't sell it to you, no matter how much money you offered". I looked at the leaf. It was not decaying in any way, the colour was glossy green, with orange and yellow reflecting in the aura of light that surrounded it. The leaf appeared newly picked from the tree, and yet it was at least five years old. I know that the energy contained within itself was keeping it alive and it was with a heavy heart that I handed it back, with the sweet melodies humming in my ear. I never felt anything so powerful from Mother Nature as that wondrous leaf. Here was another example of showing me that my Native American guide was leading the way.

My Indian has been with me for many years but now I think things are changing for me. I am seeing visions of an ancient Imperial Chinese guide. Over the last couple of years, I have felt the energy changing. Mediumship is a powerful energy, but it is invisible to many people. I would like to convert this energy so that it becomes visible. I would like to become involved in physical manifestation to ultimately prove the existence of other dimensions to everyone. I have seen table tilting and taken part in Ouija board sessions, but I am not convinced on this credibility. Both these activities require hands on intervention. They do not work without someone placing a finger on the object. True physical manifestation will not require any physical involvement, apart from mental energy. I'm not sure whether this will ever happen, but I am open to my new Chinese guide showing me the way. With this Chinese influence I am now planning on holding a Dragon Circle. I believe that my Chinese guide is working with me to bring this about. The energy of the dragon will be a powerful healing force and a power to work on a physical level. Many western Christian societies have demonised the dragon but in Far Eastern cultures like China and Japan the dragon is respected, and to have one walk beside you will bring you strength, power and good luck. **God bless my guides.**

Mother Nature

My friends Les and Jackie are vegetarians and I admire their conviction in the belief that an animal is a living gift from God and it is not for us to kill and eat. As much as I believe in the vegetarian's view point, I love my meat and can't give it up. Does this make me a bad person? I can be in the park feeding the ducks and the next night I am in the Chinese restaurant eating duck. Am I unknowingly feeding them up during the day and eating them in the evening. Maybe one day I can turn vegetarian, if not in this life then the next.

I love animals, but I'm a bit unsure of some of them. One day Les and I were drumming in a field when a heard of cows came walking towards us. I eyed them suspiciously, and when they were ten feet away it was obvious that they weren't going to stop. I grabbed my drum and shouted to Les to run. We ran out of the field and looking back, the cows had stopped to graze in the spot where we were drumming. Cows are odd creatures, I tuned into one once and all it wanted to do is eat. There really wasn't much else going on in its mind.

Another time I was walking through some fields with Les when a pony started to chase me. I ran towards a tree where I ran around and around the tree with the pony following me. The pony was obviously enjoying this game of chase and he suddenly turned to run the other way around so we crashed into one another. I fell to the ground with a bump, and the pony, acknowledging he was the victor, proudly trotted off.

I have connected with many of our pets in spirit - cats, dogs, rabbits, birds, horses. All our pets return to spirit when their days have ended. I am a believer in reincarnation. Humans have much to learn while on the earth plane. When we go home to spirit, we are assessed and if we haven't learnt all our lessons, we will be re-born on the earth plane to continue to learn and to continue our journey. What about animals? Some religions believe that humans can return as an animal if we have not led a good life while on earth. So, is that to say that an animal is a lower form of life? I don't believe so. When we have learnt our lessons, and become a pure soul, we remain in spirit and move to a higher sphere or dimension. Do animals have lessons to learn? None that I can think of, so perhaps they are the purer soul.

We all should try to look after Mother Earth, its wildlife and its plant life. I do try to be a good person, but I'm human and get it wrong. Sometimes when my pockets are full, I drop litter - normally sweet wrappers. I even try to make out it was an accident and pretend to be unaware of littering. Also, when I'm on a train and see an older person standing, I do not always offer my seat. I hide behind my newspaper, pretending I haven't seen them. I have lessons to learn in this life. Maybe in my next life I will become a road sweeper, having to pick up everyone else's litter. Perhaps I will live to a grand old age, where no one will offer me a seat in a packed train. That would be Karma. I am not perfect, far from it. I don't think anyone is perfect as there would be no reason to be here, no lessons to learn.

I love to be outside in nature. I can connect to spirit when I am at one with the earth. I can hear the whispers on the breeze and feel the energy in the wind. I am often outside with my drums, with my Native American Indian by my side. One of the best places for me to visit is Glastonbury Tor. I have made this journey many times, and I am completely at home there. I have often gone with Les, where we would hike up the Tor with our drums to sit in the old ruin at the top. When we played our rhythms and beats, the atmosphere was electric. Often people would gather up at the top of the Tor. Some bringing their own instruments, others coming to dance or sing. Fire jugglers would throw and catch their batons to the rhythm of the music. I will never forget these magical nights of music, dancing, drinking and just having a fantastic time. It was as good as any clairvoyant evening memories.

Does Money Interfere with True Spirituality?

When I'm asked to demonstrate mediumship in churches and centres I am often asked "how much do you charge?" I really don't like being asked this question, I mean how do I know until I see the number of people walking through the door. I normally ask for £15, but if only five people walk in then they probably won't have £15 in the free will offering or entrance fees. I'm happy to take less money if this is the case. On the other hand, the church or centre could have over twenty-five people in the congregation so I really should ask for more money.

Probably the fairest system I know is a church who told me that the minimum amount they would pay me is £15, but if the attendance is good, then they would be able to pay me more. There is also a centre who gives you a sealed envelope containing £20, which is a good way to avoid the "How much?" question.

No medium works in the churches and centres to make money. Let's be honest, £15 will cover the petrol expenses, and a kebab on the way home. I'm not going to make my millions here! Mediums do this type of work because they want to bring the message of spirit to the many and because they just love working with spirit.

There is quite a big difference in the price of a private reading. How much you are prepared to pay is up to you. Never judge a reading by the cost of it. You can get a fantastic reading without having to pay through the roof for it. There are brilliant mediums and psychics out there catering for all budgets.

The Jehovah's come Knocking

I invited a couple of Jehovah's Witnesses into my home when they knocked on my door one afternoon. I didn't tell them I was a spiritual medium, so they were happy and excited to discuss their way of life with me. I'm sure if they had known, they would have called me the devil and run away as fast as they could before I put a 'spell' on them.

They made themselves comfortable and we started chatting, but every time I asked a question, they would always reference the Bible. I wanted them to talk about their own feelings and views about different subjects but I could not draw them away from quoting the Bible. For instance, I agreed that the Bible was lovely, but what did they personally think about where love comes from? They didn't seem to have an answer unless it came from the Bible. This continued as I asked their opinions about war, angels, fate, hope etc. They appeared to not have a personal opinion on any subject and continued to quote the Bible.

Well everyone who knows me knows I can talk for England, and those Jehovah's Witnesses could not get out of the house. The reverse was in play here, normally when Jehovah's Witnesses come knocking we hide behind our closed doors, or on answering the door, close it rather quickly so we don't have to talk to them. I was quite happy to chat. We had a very interesting conversation but after two hours they were itching to leave. They kept looking at their watch and eventually announced that it was dinner time and that they really did need to leave. I invited them back later to finish our conversation as I really enjoyed it. They left saying they would definitely be back. I'm still waiting for them to return!

Spiritual churches and centres welcome all faiths through their doors. They are not there to convert anyone to change their faith, only to accept that there is eternal life - a life beyond this earthly presence which is open to everyone. I personally have a great interest in other beliefs and cultures. I often read books about other faiths and my findings are that with most faiths there is a belief to lead a happy, respectful and a caring life - to help those less fortunate then yourself and to be mindful of your actions. Angels seem to appear in most faiths. These wonderful, powerful beings may be the link to peace among us all.

How the World of Spirit Works

I was watching a demonstration by Roy Jones when he gave a message to a lady in the congregation. Roy said that the spirit he was connected to was learning about life through her and her experiences. I fully believe that when we return home to spirit, our learning continues. We may be going through a difficulty that the spirit had never experienced. Watching how we cope or deal with the experience, enlightens spirit and the knowledge gained will help them when they are re-born onto the earth plane. Our journeys are continuous until all our lessons are learned. Only then can we rise to the higher levels or dimensions of spirit world. My mother once brought my paternal grandmother to a spiritualist church. She felt very uncomfortable in the church and couldn't wait to leave. She had no understanding of spirit and felt too frightened to find out. She was also quite introvert and a very private person, and the thought of the medium giving her a message in front of everyone filled her with terror. She never returned to the church again. I often feel her close when I am working and I believe she is learning all she can from me about my spiritual journey in readiness for her return. Perhaps she will return as a fantastic medium or perhaps she will just allow herself to be a bit more outgoing and not so fearful of the world around her.

Spirit are also given work to do. A client of mine mentioned that another medium told her that her mother was busy helping children cross over from earth to spirit. While on the earth plane her mother was a foster carer, so this makes total sense.

Family in spirit can also influence and guide us to meet the right people at the right time. They can present opportunities that will be of help to us. Whether we take any notice of the people who cross our paths, or to take the opportunities presented to us, is another matter. We all have free will and can act or disregard as we see fit.

Reincarnation

Some spiritualists do not believe in reincarnation. They believe that this is it, you get one life and then return home to spirit. I don't agree with them. Why don't I agree? Well we are born on earth to experience many ways of life and to learn many lessons and you can't possibly experience everything there is to learn in one life. There is just too much. Although I have gone through many things, surely, I've got to experience other types of life's emotions and concepts.

I once gave a reading where I connected with the clients great, great, grandfather who died on the Titanic, which raises the question that if reincarnation takes place, how can a medium connect to a spirit of so many generations back. I believe that only a part of your soul is re-born to earth, the residue remains in spirit. When you return to spirit again you join with the residue that remained, to make a whole again. This whole soul has now experienced many lives and the cycle will continue until all lessons are learnt. We would then move to a higher sphere or dimension. Although some of my teachers have stated that all of your soul returns. My argument is how can a medium connect to someone in spirit if all of the soul is back on earth?

It's difficult for us to imagine this, but spirit is an energy and that energy is a power within our earthly soul and our spirit soul. Being in dream state is the nearest I can come to explaining the energy. When we dream we know it is not a solid form, it is like an energy. Having said that, whenever I see spirit with my psychical eye, they appear as solid form. So, spirit can appear to us as energy, form or dream-like.

Another question I am always asked is "How big is the spirit world. It must be full to overflowing with all the spirits - human and animal." The trouble is that they are gaging the world of spirit against the earth plane. They are looking at it in 3D, but the world of spirit is eternal, never ending. Spirit is an energy with no solid form. When you have crossed over to the other side, you will be able to see your friends and family, but they will appear dream-like.

It is a very complex subject and now made even more complex as Quantum Physics researchers are saying that time overlaps and you could possibly be living in two parallel lives – with another making different decisions and walking a very different path to the one you are walking now. That's taking reincarnation to the extreme which leads me to think that perhaps the soul would need to divide into the two parallel lives.

This is all way too deep for me or this book. I trust in what I know and believe to be true, although I always keep an open mind for other theories. I am always ready to discuss and learn more about spirit and other dimensions.

Shamanic and Pagan Teaching

I enjoy running circles, workshops and shamanic events. A few years ago, I bought a piece of land with a mud hut on it which gave me the opportunity to run more of these events. When the weather is good I hold the events outside, often building a fire for everyone to sit round. In the winter I use the mud hut where we light the log burner.

When I first acquired the land, the first thing I had to do was repair the holes in the hut roof. Now I'm not the most practical of men. My DIY skills are virtually non-existent, and according to my girlfriend, watching me trying to fix the roof was the best 'Frank Spencer' moment she had ever seen. She giggled the whole time I was up there. My arms and legs just couldn't find co-ordination and I nearly fell off numerous times. After a number of attempts the roof finally got fixed ready for my winter events.

Les Fuller is a fantastic shamanic teacher. We have been holding shamanic workshops for quite a while now and have created a little community who attend as often as they can. These workshops are all about learning the shamanic way by working with nature, healing, drumming, chanting and learning about our spirit animals. There is a real closeness within the group. People tell me they feel uplifted after the workshop and that there is a 'feel-good' factor when experiencing the different aspects to the workshop. One lady told me that she worked in an office all week and coming to the workshop leaves her feeling refreshed, even if it is held in the hut when the weather is bad. The donkeys from the donkey sanctuary are often drawn to the sound of our drumming, and peer over the fence at us as if they are wanting to join in. We can often hear the screeching of buzzards flying overhead. There is a real sense of being with one in nature.

We also hold pagan workshops which focus on singing and healing. These tend to be held during the winter so take place in the hut. Les will play a flute while everyone sings old English music songs. Again, there is a real closeness to the group, everyone goes home feeling at peace. ***God bless my little sanctuary.***

A Message Retold

The following story was written by Carole Long who had recorded a message I gave her while demonstrating at the Beacon of Light Spiritualist Church.

My son, Simon, left for university in August 2014 and I was missing him terribly, worrying for him, and wanting him to have everything he needed. Clearly my son was enjoying his freedom having been in the family with a restricted social life due to his older sister being disabled - so no late nights or noisy parties! Given he now had the opportunity to buy his own drinks, I was concerned about how he would control himself and worried he would get blindly drunk!

In October 2014 Jeff was demonstrating at The Beacon of Light. At that time, I was on the committee and busy helping during the service, so clearly wasn't expecting or even hoping to get a message. Jeff came to me, at first rather reluctantly as he knew I was on the committee, but his connection with my father was absolutely brilliant. I recall it very clearly as follows:

"A gentleman comes through who says he is dad, father, and he is talking about Simon. Simon is here on the

earth plane. He's saying that you are worried about Simon. Not big concerns but a slight worry, like will he ever be able to cope with something! Do you understand that? – (bit of laughter) – but dad is saying, Simon will be alright, he will be alright. I'll be beside him, I'll be beside him. Dad says you want to phone him up all the time – "Simon are you alright?" and it's only gone like a couple of hours before you are on the phone again to him – "Simon?" – (laughter from Jeff) – "have you got your jimjams?" You should understand this conversation – um – and you're on the phone again "Have you got enough socks?" It's like you have to go through every single item. "Don't forget to brush your teeth" (all laughing). Your dad says Simon is going to be ok, and he says it's about time Simon did his own thing – alright? It's a bit like he is flying the nest. He's got to learn somehow to cope on his own. Your dad was saying what a bright lad he is. Ok, take his love, and I want to give you the name John (dad's name) and I say God bless."

Just as Jeff was about to leave me he came back and said

"Dad's still here and he says it doesn't matter what I say she'll still phone him tonight! He says it's no good saying it Jeff, she'll still ring him and worry. You are worried that Simon will drink too much!" (Lots of laughter) "Don't worry, he won't be drinking."

So yes, I was concerned about Simon's drinking, particularly through the freshers week! A few days later I got a call from my son. He had to go to hospital as he had broken his ankle jumping down some steps on his way to a night out where he had planned to get completely pickled! For the next six weeks Simon had to struggle around with his foot in a plaster cast and on crutches. He was prevented from joining in the freshers week and had to get his head down to study instead! So, my dad's message, saying he would be by his side and keep an eye on him and his drinking was absolutely spot on – clearly the only way to prevent it was a broken ankle!

Sometimes the simplest of messages is enough evidence to give a positive and uplifting path forward in someone's life, as told here:

"When I first saw Jeff at Walthamstow Spiritualist Church, I thought he was a loon and a fake! But, at the end of the service he came to me and gave me a reading. He had connected with my uncle who had died at the age of 43, of a heart attack. My uncle and I weren't speaking at the time of his death but Jeff's message from him has always stuck with me. Jeff told me everything that had happened to cause the upset, and he said that my uncle needs to say sorry and make his peace with me. I just broke down in tears. That wonderful and meaningful message has always remained

with me and I will never forget it. It enabled me to move on with my life knowing that my uncle walked beside me."

Happiness

Sometimes you have to wait a while to find your happiness. Life can be a struggle or upsetting, but from time to time you have to experience 'not-so-happy' events and feelings to know and acknowledge happiness. The saying 'things happen for a reason' is very true. When life throws us into turmoil or grief it is difficult for us to understand why it has happened. Whether it was a family upset, a relationship ending or losing a job, these things and many other life changes that are very upsetting are our life lessons. Spirit needs us to know many different experiences and feelings in order to move forward, gain wisdom and have empathy for others in similar circumstances. I was once asked why spirit would want a man to lose his job and home which resulted in him being homeless. I believe that lessons are to be learned and experienced to enable us to grow in spirit. And when we are re-born to the earth plane, spirit will put us in a position where we can draw on past life lessons to help ourselves, to help others and to live a happy life. That may not be very comforting for the man who is sleeping on the pavement in the middle of winter, but perhaps another soul who was homeless themselves in a previous life will be devoted to bringing about changes, to clothe, feed and find shelter to those in need in this life.

Losing a loved one to spirit is devasting but know that life continues in a world where there is no pain, and unconditional love flows eternal. To lose a child to spirit is probably the most difficult to understand. If spirit is love why would they take a child away from a loving family? Children need to live a childhood in the beautiful world of spirit. They will live and grow within spirit's love, without sadness and never knowing what it is to suffer. Of course, the child's mother and father are suffering dreadfully, but for whatever the reasons, happiness awaits on this earth plane and the next.

Do everything you can that makes you happy. Keep loving people around you. Give more than you take. Dance like nobody is watching and sing like nobody is listening. Don't take life too seriously. Try not to take offence too easily. Make happiness your goal! Your laughter and happiness will flow from you, to touch and heal others who come within your space. When you are feeling down, look for the little things that you can feel grateful for, that you are happy to have in your life. Just food on your plate and a roof - no matter how small - over your head.

I love my life! I do not own a big home nor do I drive a flashy car (actually, I feel very lucky every time my car engine starts, given the age of it!). I do not take exotic holidays nor do I eat in upmarket restaurants. I need very little in this materialistic world. I'm grateful to have a roof over my head and food in my tummy, but above all else I'm so grateful to be Happy!

*****

Have Fun!

Be Happy!

Love Life!

Printed in Poland
by Amazon Fulfillment
Poland Sp. z o.o., Wrocław